꽃 피는 그리움

Longing blooms like a flower

꽃 피는 그리움

펴낸날 | 2021년 11월 15일 초판 1쇄

지은이 | 강현국
펴낸이 | 강현국
펴낸곳 | 도서출판 시와반시

등록 | 2011년 10월 21일 등록(제25100-2011-000034호)
주소 | 대구광역시 수성구 지산로 14길 83, 101-2408호
전화 | 053) 654-0027
전자우편 | khguk92@hanmail.net

ISBN 978-89-8345-124-8   03800

값 15,000원

First edition on November 15, 2021.

Written by Hyun-Guk Kang
Publishing by Hyun-Guk Kang
Published by the Poetry and Anti-poetry

Registered on October 21, 2011 (No. 25100-2011-000034)
Address: 101-2408, Jisan-ro 14-gil 83, Suseong-gu, Daegu City
Representative call: 053-654-0027, Fax 053-622-0377
E-mail: khguk92@hanmail.net

ISBN 978-89-8345-124-8   03800

꽃 피는 그리움
Longing blooms like a flower

강현국 디카시집

Dicapoems by Hyun-Guk Kang

시와반시

'몸 밖까지 환한 풍경'으로 하려다가
'꽃 피는 그리움'으로 이름을 바꾸었다.
사유와 이미지의 가지런한 몸매를 위해서였다.

풍경의 그리움, 그리움의 풍경이여!
꿈꾸는 거기, 먼 곳에 이르도록 다정하기를…

2021년 가을 강현국

Poet's words.

I was going to do it with 'Bright Scenery to the outside of my
body',
The name was changed to 'Longing blooms like a flower'.
It was for a neat appearance of thought and image.

The longing of scenery, the scenery of longing!
I hope you'll be kind enough to reach far away from your
dream…

Fall 2021. Hyun-Guk Kang

차례

제1부　내 삶의 객지　Part 1 Place far away from home

제2부 별빛이 지은 둥지   **Part 2** Starlight Nest

제4부 저 구름 흘러가는 곳 Part 4 Where the clouds flow

내 삶의 객지

Place far away from home

어디 있니?
Where are you?

어디 있니?
잠든다 해도 꽃이 피는
뜬눈으로 찾고 있는 너 지금 어디 있니?

Where are you?
Even if I sleep, flowers bloom
I'm looking for you with my eyes open. Where are
you right now?

빈자의 지갑
Poor man's wallet

그리움을 찾아 그리움의 끝까지 간다 해도, 이제 그만!
악수를 청하는 그리움은 거기 없네. 거기 없는 그리움만
거기 가득 출렁일 뿐.

Even if you go to the end of longing in search of
longing, stop now!
The longing to ask for a handshake is not there. Only
the longing that's not there flutters there.

쏜살같이
Like a shot

어느덧
술잔을 엎지르듯 한 생生을 엎질렀네!

엎지르진 한 생生이 막차를 타고
다시 못 올 먼 곳으로 쏜살같이 떠나가네!

A short time
I spilled a life like spilled a glass of wine!

A life of spilt-upness took the last train
He is going off to a far place can't come back

마음이 아파
I'm broken-hearted

비 온다 해도, 우산 들고
나 거기 갈 수 없네.

너무 멀어서

너 여기 올 수 없네.
꽃 핀다 해도, 김밥 들고

Even if it rains, I'll hold an umbrella
I can't go there.

It's too far

You can't come here.
Even if flowers bloom, I'll hold gimbap
When the body is distant from the mind, when the
mind is unfamiliar with the body
When I miss me

당신은 어디 있는지
Where are you?

저무는 서산이 잠시 환한 것은
새들이 데리고 온 하늘
노동의 푸른 쇠스랑 때문입니다.

지하철 한구석에 먹다 만 컵라면을 두고 간 당신,
당신은 어디 있는지?

Shortly brightens up in getting dark west mountain
The sky brought by the birds
Because of the blue pitchfork of labor.

You left your cup noodle in the corner of the subway.
Where are you?

이별

Farewell

비바람 잦았지만 우리 오래 행복했다.

늙은 애비 버리고 미련 없이 떠나거라!

멀리멀리, 낯선 세상 참 푸르기도 하지.

Rain and wind were frequent, but we were happy for

a long time.

Leave your old father and leave without regret!

Far away, far away, an unfamiliar world is so blue.

아무런 방해도 받지 않는
Not disturbed by anything

이것 아닌 것도 없고 저것 아닌 것도 없는 것으로 가득한
저쪽 아닌 것도 없고 이쪽 아닌 것도 없는 것으로 적막한
이 세상 양지만이 아니라 저세상 음지까지 닿아서 눈
부신

Filled with everything that's not this and that
Still with nothing that's not here and nothing that's
not there
Bright not just from the world's sunny side but to the
world's dark side

가려움

Itch

마음 없는 몸이 허깨비이듯
몸 없는 마음 또한 믿을 것이 못 된다.

한 많은 사연들이 닥지닥지 달라붙어 한 세상이 가렵다.

As if a body without a heart is a ghost
The mind without the body is also unbelievable.

One world is itchy with so many stories sticking together.

밥
Eat

간발의 차로 남의 처가 된 첫사랑처럼 어리석은 생이여!
떠난 당신을 다시 보내고 혼자 밥을 먹는다.

A foolish life like the first love who became someone
else's wife by accident!
Let you go again after you've left and eating alone.

구석의 메아리

Echo in the corner

절벽과 부딪쳐 깨어지는 구석의 맨주먹 그래, 나는 구석
의 메아리였지.
구석진 내 몸엔 잔소리처럼 비가 새고 흐린 등불은 자
주 꺼졌지.

A bare fist in the corner that hits a cliff and breaks,
yeah,
I was an echo in the corner.
Rain leaked out like a nag and the cloudy lanterns
were often extinguished.

어깨동무

The friendly arms

우리라는 말의 다정한 어깨동무!
애썼다, 수고했다, 고맙고 미안하다. 저기 저 발자국들에
게 그렇게 말해야지.

The friendly arms of the word we!
Good job, thank you and sorry. You have to say that
to those footprints.

칠흑의 불꽃

The darkest flame in the world

떠나던 슬픔이 가던 길 멈추고 되돌아볼 때, 망자를 독수
리에게 보내는 그 순간은 참혹하고 황량하고 쓸쓸하기도
합니다. 하지만 어느 죽음인들 참혹하고 황량하고 쓸쓸
하지 않을 수 있겠습니까.

When the sorrow of leaving stops and looks back on
its way, the moment of sending the dead to the eagle
is devastating, desolate, and lonely. But which of the
dead might not be desolate and lonely.

저승길처럼

Like the road of afterlife

가다가 쉬어가는 저승길처럼
추우면 어깨를 맞대기도 하면서
우리 여기까지 왔네!

Going and resting like the road of afterlife
When it's cold, we put our shoulders together
We've come all the way here!

푸른 빙벽
Blue ice wall

바닥이 헤진 아이젠을 신고 하필이면
푸른 빙벽의 이마를 가진 당신을 만났으니

가면을 벗기 위해 가면을 쓰는 삶의 비애!
풍자가 슬픈 이유이다.

Why would I wear a worn-out izen
Now that I've met you with a blue ice wall on your
forehead

Sadness of wearing a mask to take off the mask!
That's why satire is sad.

기도

Prayer

나 혼자 편안한 몰염치의 식탁과 버릇처럼 날뛰는 후안
무치와 파렴치의 일상을 뉘우치게 하소서.

Let me repent of the daily life of shyness and shame,
comfortable table enjoyed alone run around like a
habit.

한적한 오후다
불타는 오후다
더 없을 것이 없는
오후다
나는 나무속에서
자온다 —오규원—

한 시절
One time

누구에게나 한 시절은 무거운 한 시절이다.

나란히 앉아 보낸 한 시절이라 하더라도

가벼운 한 시절은 어디에도 없다.

A time for everyone is a heavy time.

Even though it was a time when we sat side by side

There is no light a time anywhere.

가뭇하다

Far apart

세상은 나를 버렸으나

나는 세상을 버리지 않았으니

玄

玄

玄

玄

각진 모서리가 둥글어지기까지

당신과 나 사이 가뭇하다.

The world has abandoned me

But I didn't abandon the world

玄

玄

玄

玄

Until the edges become round.

You and I are very far apart.

노래는 무얼 먹고 사는가?

What does a song eat?

구름은 구름끼리
허공에 기대어 허공을 노래한다.

노래는 어디에서 잠자고 무얼 먹고 사는가.
아무리 생각해도 쓸쓸한 생이여!

하늘의 높이는 배고픔의 깊이이다.

Clouds between clouds
Sing the air Leaning in the air.

Where do songs sleep and what do they eat.
No matter how much I think about it, it's a lonely life!

The height of the sky is the depth of hunger.

왜? 대답이 없습니까?

Why? You got no answer?

신은 죽었다, 신은 죽었다!

죽은 신이 나뭇잎을 떨구는 동안

회색 위에 검정

왜? 대답이 없습니까?

당신에게 우리는 누구입니까?

God is dead, God is dead!

While the dead gods dropped the leaves

Black on gray

Why? You got no answer?

Who are we to you?

두려움

Fear

삶이란

끈으로 묶을 수 없는 두려운 낭떠러지

Life is

A dreadful cliff that cannot be tied with a string

마른 잎 허공

A dry leaf air

나는 한때 햇볕 잘 드는 허공 위에

젖은 양말 여러 켤레 얹어둔 적 있다.

길 없는 길 위에서 오래 헤매었다.

On a sunny air

I once put several pairs of wet socks on top.

I wandered for a long time on the road without a road.

무슨 관계란 말인가
What's the relationship

뵈르소가 방아쇠를 당겼다. 파리와 가려움은 항상 존재
하기 마련이다. 그래서 인생은 살기가 어려운 것이다. 총
소리가 허공을 찢었다. 한참을 있다가 내 마음 안쪽이 피
에 젖었다. 하얀 수도원과 홀로 빛나는 새벽별이 무슨 관
계란 말인가!

Mörso pulled the trigger. Flies and itching always ex-
ist. That's why life is hard to live. The sound of the gun
ripped through the air. After a long time, the inside of
my heart was soaked in blood. What's the relationship
between a white monastery and a shining dawn star!

빨간 자동차

A red car

빈집 마당은 빈집 마당으로, 오고 가는 아침은 오고 가는 아침으로 저렇듯 초연하다.
하늘에 떠 있는 구름의 한평생은 구름의 한평생을 걱정하지 않는다.
오로지 빨간 자동차가 빈집 초연을 낯설어 한다. 시동을 끄지 않았기 때문이리라.

The empty house yard is an empty house yard, and the morning that comes and goes is the morning that comes and goes. so they are as silent as that.
One lifetime of clouds floating in the sky does not worry about one lifetime of clouds.
Only red car is unfamiliar with the being quiet of empty houses. Because he didn't turn off the engine.

손
Hand

마침내 내 육신마저도 하룻밤 쉬어가는 여인숙일 뿐이
라고 기억 밖으로 밀어내는 손, 궂은 비 오는 날 나 떠난
다 하더라도 그저 생각 없이 먼 산을 바라보기만 할 손,
"이제 내 할 일 없어졌군" 하며 두 손을 탁탁 털고 나면
그만인 손.

Finally, a hand that pushes even my body that is only
just a restful inn out of memory, a hand that just looks
at a distant mountain without thinking even if I leave
on a rainy day, and a hand that shakes off both hands,
saying, "I have nothing to do now."

그대들도 행복하세요!

I wish you happiness, too!

나는 행복합니다.

그대들도 행복하세요!

2005년 4월 그날 추기경 한 분이 흰 구름 그림자 두고 가셨다.

딱따구리가 천상의 악기를 다듬는 마른 가지 저 너머로 가셨다.

이 세상의 저자가 누구인지 알 것 같다.

I am happy.

I wish you happiness, too!

On that day in April 2005, a cardinal left behind a white cloud shadow.

He went beyond the dry branches where a woodpecker refine the heavenly

instrument.

I think I know who the author of this world is.

별빛이 지은 둥지

Starlight Nest

일자무식
Ignorance

숟가락도 없이, 노란 새 한 마리가 커다랗게 내려앉아 아침 식사를 하고 있었네. 식사는 끼니가 아니라 삶의 이유라는 듯이 호수에 비친 제 그림자를 들여다보며 지극히 목소리를 가다듬었네, 햇볕이 지은 밥 무상으로 먹었으니 무상으로 노래 불러 각진 시간의 모서리를 부드럽게 펴는 것도 잊지 않았네.

일자무식의 이 넉넉함!

Without a spoon, a yellow bird was sitting big and eating breakfast. As if eating is not a meal but a reason for life, She looked into her shadow reflected in the lake and refined her voice. Since she ate rice cooked by the sun free of charge, she didn't forget to sing for free and spread the corners of the sharp time.

What a abundance of ignorance!

가을 호수

Autumn lake

고독은 노란색, 외로움은 파란색, 서러움은 붉은색. 물
속에 가라앉은 가을 숲 좀 봐, 얼마나 서늘한 노래를 부
르는지!

Solitude is yellow, loneliness is blue, sadness is red.
Look at the autumn forest sunken in the water, what a
cool song it sings!

물방울
Water drop

돌담의 적막과
봄날의 그리움이 밀어올린 환한! 물방울.

천사의 눈빛.

Bright! water drop
By the silence of the stone wall and the longing for
spring pushed up.

Angel eyes.

오월

May

인디언의 오월은 오래전에 죽은 자를 생각하는 달

오래전에 죽은 자를 데리고 호수 속에 갈앉아 처연한 버
드나무
할 일 없는 그리움이 잔잔한 물결로 자지러진다.
기약 없는 이별이, 다시 만날 이별에게 악수를 청하는 레
퀴엠처럼

Indian May is the month of remembrance of those
who died long ago

A gloomy willow tree that sat down in the lake with
the dead long ago
The longing for nothing to do is broken down in a
calm wave.
A farewell without promise, like a requiem asking for
a handshake to a farewell we will meet again

오솔길
Trail

오솔길이 오솔길을 따라 산속에 들듯 단풍은 제 몸의 열기로 제 갈 길을 만든다. 꽃 피고 새 우는 것도 우주의 리듬이니 바위 틈 오솔길은 신발이 필요 없고 담쟁이 일생은 잡념이 없다. 가을밤 독주毒酒처럼, 저 산 너머 떨어지는 별똥별처럼.

Just as the trail goes into the mountains along the trail, the autumn leaves make a way for him with the heat of his body. Blooming flowers and singing birds are also the rhythms of the universe, so a trail between rocks does not require shoes, and an ivy's life is free of distractions. Like a strong liquor drink on an autumn night, like a shooting star falling over that mountain.

연애
Love

구름을 목에 두른 늙은 소나무가 산안개 자욱 명상에 잠
길 때, 주민등록증도 없는 기러기 가족이 조그만 개울가
에서 늦잠을 즐길 때, 개똥지빠귀가 가장 깊은 숲속에 제
집을 짓기 위해 계곡물소리를 물어 나를 때, 길 떠나는
다람쥐 부부가 하루분의 김밥을 쌀 때, 내가 사물과 연
애 중일 때

그 아침은 눈이 부셔 12345가 보이지 않는다.

When an old pine with clouds around its neck is im-
mersed in the mist of meditation, when a family of
geese without a national ID card overslept by a small
creek, when a thrush carry the sound of a stream to
build its own house in the deepest forest, when leaving the road when a squirrel couple wraps a day's
kimbap, when I'm in love with things

The morning is dazzling and 12345 is invisible.

생명에 대해

About life

그가 왔다!

마침내 어느 먼 별나라에서?

소문도 없이 그가 와서

내겐 해종일 지진이 일었다.

꽃의 눈부심이여!

He came!

Finally, in some distant star?

Without a word he came

There have been earthquakes all year long for me.

The glare of flowers!

첫눈 와요!
First snow!

첫눈 와요!

온 세상 열어젖힌 유리창 속에
물들인 군복과 동성로 낱담배와
당신이 그리웠던 주막집이 갇힌다.

First snow!

In the open windows of the whole world
Dyed military uniforms and Dongseongro single
cigarettes
The tavern you missed is trapped.

초록 악기

Green instruments

몸 낮추어 귀 기울이면 네 목소리 들린다.

안녕! 옥수수 영감님

초록 악기가 부르는 슬픈 아다지오.

If you lower your body and listen, you can hear your
voice.

Hi! corn boss

Sad Adagio sung by green instruments.

발자국

Footprints

누군가 물 위를 걸어간 발자국 같은
누군가 말을 타고 물 위를 달려간 발자국 같은
뒤쫓던 내 마음이 물에 흘려 못 박힌 발자국 같은…

Like the footprints of someone walking on the water
Like the footprints of someone riding a horse and
running on the water
My heart that was chasing is like footprints be nailed
to the water…

허공
The air

허공의 힘으로 새들은 날고, 새들의 힘으로 허공은 푸르러 하늘이 된다.
열쇠를 들고 열쇠를 찾는 그대
까마득한 허공에 아픈 어깨를 묻어보라. 푸른 하늘이 아픈 그대 어깨 날개가 될 때까지.

With the power of the air, the birds fly, and with the power of the birds, the air becomes blue and the sky.
You holding the key and looking for the key
Bury your sore shoulder in the dark air. Until the blue sky becomes the wings of your sore shoulder.

나무
Tree

대지의 우람한 근육을 보라. 뿌리에 새겨진 상처를 보라.
인고의 세월이 피운 꽃이 이쁘다!

그것이 인생이다.

Look at the thick muscles of the earth. Look at the
wounds carved into the roots. What a beautiful the
flowers that have bloomed through times of hard
work are!

That's life.

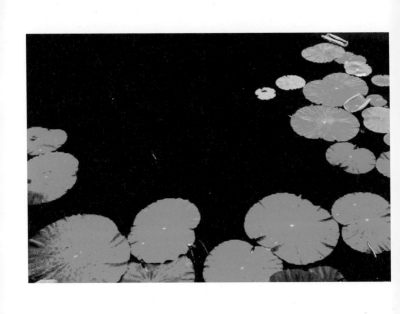

산책

Take a walk

마음속 풍경을 천천히 걸어보라. 모자는 벗어두고 명아주 지팡이를 짚는 게 좋겠지. 오솔길 끝자락에 호수가 있고, 입술이 붉은 물총새 둥지 곁에 아랫목이 따뜻한 초가집이 있겠지. 마음속 풍경을 거니노라면 돈으로 살 수 없는 날의 행복이 맨발로 달려 나와 오랜만이야! 눈인사를 걸어오겠지.

Walk slowly through the landscape in your mind. It would be better to take off your hat and use a cane. There's a lake at the end of the trail, and a thatched cottage with a warm room next to the red-lipped kingfisher's nest. If I walk through the scenery in my heart, the happiness of days that money can't buy runs barefoot! It's been a long time! say hello with eyes

별이 빛나는 밤
Starry night

별빛 새끼들 만나러 가야겠다. 실눈 같던 메뚜기들 많이 자랐겠다. 감꽃 진지 오래이니 사마귀 앞발이 튼튼해졌겠다. 한 고요가 벌떡 일어나 한 고요의 따귀를 때릴 듯 별이 빛나는 밤, 아무도 없는 거기 독주 한잔하러 가야겠다.

I have to go see the starlight cubs. There must have been grown a lot of locusts that looked like thin eyes. It's been a long time since the persimmon blossoms, so the mantis' front paws must have gotten stronger. On a starry night, as if a stillness would rise up and slap a stillness, I should go no one there for a glass of whiskey.

나뭇잎 법고法鼓
Dharma leaves

아픈 세상을 어루만지고, 막힌 세상을 두드리고, 구석진
세상을 멀리멀리 폈다. 잃어버린 시간을 어루만지고, 잃
어버린 시간의 벽을 두드리고, 검은 시간의 골짜기를 환
하게 폈다. 낙엽이 지기 전에

He touched the sick world, beaten up the closed
world, and spread the cornered world far away. He
touched lost time, beaten up the wall of lost time, and
opened up the dark valley of time. Before he falls

꽃의 숭고

A flower's noble

꽃의 일생은 당당함으로 숭고하다.

A flower's life is noble with pride.

나팔꽃 창밖
Outside the window of the morning glory

나팔꽃은 새벽 창밖에 매달려
팔팔하고 씩씩하다. 기죽지 않고…
깨어진 창밖이 제 집이기 때문이다.

The morning glory hangs outside the window
He's lively and energetic. He won't be discouraged…
Because the broken window is his home.

눈 뜨는 소리

Awaenking sounds

고요한 산사에 적막이 놀러 왔다. 풍경이 울었다. 허공이
눈 뜨는 소리 멀리멀리 들렸다.

The silence came to the quiet temple. The wind bell
cried. I could hear the sound of air opening his eyes
far away.

해맑은 응시

The bright staring

저렇듯 해맑은 응시를 보라. 서역 하늘까지 뒤꿈치가 환
한 새벽 풀밭은 산 첩첩 물 중중
당신의 구불구불 속마음을 이미 알아챘다는 눈치이다.

Look at the bright staring like that. The early morning grass whose heels are bright to the western sky
seems to have already noticed your crooked inside
heart.

새뽀얗게 멎었다

It stopped bright

술렁대던 두근거림이 새뽀얗게 멎었다.

The trembling heart stopped bright.

스스로 허공

The air of one's own accord

과일은 향기로 자신이 있던 들판과 자신의 몸에 물을 뿌려준 비와 자신이 보았던 저녁노을에 대해 이야기한다. (세잔)

허공은 달과 나무의 전생을 이미 알아챘다는 눈치다. 발효와 숙성의 시간을 건너온 자재自在, '스스로 그렇게 있음'의 경지이다.

Fruits talk about the fields they were in with scents, the rain that sprayed water on their bodies, and the sunset they saw(Paul Cezanne)

The air seems to have already recognized the past life of the moon and trees. It is a place where materials that have crossed the time of fermentation and ripening are "so on their own."

고요의
남쪽
Southern Calm

얼마나 멀리로부터

How far away are you from?

뒤뜰 모란은 달빛이 피워 올린 땅의 문자이다. 그 향기 얼마나 멀리 가는지, 얼마나 멀리! 로부터, 끝없는 흐름 속에 몽롱하게 사라지는 내 노래의 영토로부터 너울너울 날아드는 호랑나비 부부를 보라. 당신을 꽃피우는 허공의 춤은 얼마나 아름다운지.

A backyard peony is a text of the land lit by moonlight. How far the scent goes, how far! from. See the tiger butterfly couple fluttering away from the territory of my song, which disappears in an endless stream. What a beautiful dance in the air that blooms you.

우산
Umbrella

젖지 않는 어깨는 아늑하다.
아늑한 어깨는 환하게 꽃 핀다.
먼 곳으로부터 말 달려온
그대라는 마음의 우산이 있어.

그러니 신이여, 비를 뿌리려거든 단비를 뿌리소서.
(숫타니파타)

The shoulders that don't get wet are cozy.
Cozy shoulders blossom brightly.
There's an umbrella who horses running from far
away.
In my heart called you.

So god, if you want to sprinkle rain, sprinkle sweet
rain." (Sutanipata)

통나무집 부근

Near the log cabin

계곡물소리 맨발로 모여들고

초록의 길 하나 환하게 열리는

눈 내려도 얼지 않는 영혼의 집

The sound of the water in the valley gathers with bare
feet

One green road opens brightly

A soul home that doesn't freeze even when it snows

홀로 놀다
Play alone

초록의 환희는 동튼 새벽같이 조용히 다가온다.

처음에 존재했고, 지금 존재하고, 그리고 항상 존재할 그
림자처럼.

The green joy comes quietly like dawn.

Like a shadow that existed in the beginning, is now,
and will always be.

세월의 간이역

Whistle stop station of Time

.

외로움의 거처
Home of loneliness

미안하구나, 빛나는 반야여
외롭기 위해 사는 것이 아니라 사는 것이 외로운 것임을!

I'm sorry, shining Sutra
I don't live to be lonely, but to live is to be lonely!

기우뚱한 폐허

Sloppy ruins

지게 목발 두드리던 늙은 애비 노래 속 불쌍한 내 새끼 세
상 끝 어디에서 흔들리고 있는지.
무너질 듯 기우뚱한 폐허의 주홍 글씨!

Where my poor baby is shaking at the end of the
world in the song of old father who was tapping on
Jige crutches.
The scarlet letters of the ruins that lean as if they are
about to collapse!

변방

Periphery

아무래도 변방이란, 아랫목에 누워서도 손 시린 땅, 어느새 내가 여기까지 왔구나! 모락모락 김이 나는 한숨의 영토이다.

I guess the periphery is the land where my hands are cold even when I lie down on the warm part of the room, and I've come all the way here! It is a territory of sigh that steams up.

북극성 입구

North Star entrance

빨랫줄로부터 밤하늘까지는 도저히 닿을 수 없다는 펄럭이는 옥양목 치마의 한탄 때문이었을 것이다. 그녀가 쑥과 마늘을 토해내고 도로 곰이 되었으면 좋겠다고 맞장구친 까닭은 동굴 속을 빠져나온 작은곰자리의 맨발이 먼 북극성의 입구이리라는 더듬거리는 판단 때문이었을 것이다.

It must have been due to the lamentation of a Ok-yangmok skirt that could never reach the night sky from the clothesline. The reason why she hoped to vomit mugwort and garlic and come back to the bear must have been because of the fumbling judgment that bare feet of the Little Bear that escaped the cave would be the entrance to the distant North Star.

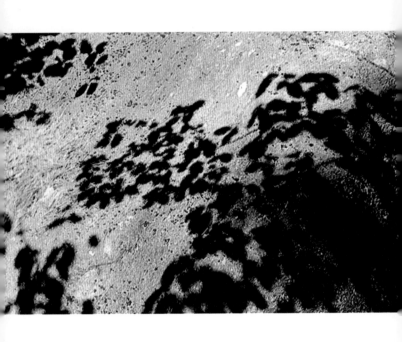

생의 의지
Will of life

기록이란 소멸의 항체, 생의 의지이다. 기록은 단단해서 시간을 비끼고, 그 빛은 찬란해서 천지를 비추나 한 시절의 주인은 그곳에 없다.

Records are the antibody of extinction and the will to live. The records are solid, so they miss time, and the light is brilliant and shines on heaven and earth, but the owner of the time is not there.

돌담길

Stone wall road

돌담길을 걷노라면 나를 부르는 잃어버린 어머니 목소
리 저 멀리서 들려오는 듯도 하고, 주름진 왼손이 언뜻
언뜻 주름진 오른손을 아주 낯설게 바라보는 듯도 한다.
두 손이 움켜쥔 세월의 풍상을 누구라서 쉬이 빠져나갈
수 있단 말인가!

Walking along the stone wall road, the lost voice of
my mother calling me seems to be heard from a far,
and my wrinkled left hand seems to look very strange
at first glance at the wrinkled right hand. Who can
easily escape the suffering of time that their hands
have grabbed!

곰삭은 기억
Mulled memories

그것이 비록 딱딱한 악성종양이라 하더라도 세월은 모든
기억을 곰삭힌다. 곰삭은 기억은 가지를 뻗고 검은 허공
을 푸르게 덮는다. 곰삭은 기억으로부터 우리는 하나이
고 곰삭은 기억으로부터 세계는 가볍다.

Even if it is a hard malignant tumor time mulls all
memories. The mulled memories stretch branches
and cover the black air blue. We are one from the
mulled memory and the world is light from the mulled
memory.

쓸쓸한 풍경

Lonely landscape

"마음을 바쳐 어떤 현실을 사랑하자마자 그것은 벌써 혼이 되고 추억이 되어버린다."라고 바슐라르는 쓰고 있다. 어느덧 황혼, 참 쓸쓸한 풍경이다. 어쩔 수 없이 나는 한 시절의 부재, 그 숨 막히는 공허의 춤을 추어보는 것이다.

"As soon as you give my heart to love a reality, it already becomes a soul and a memory." writes Bachelard. It's already twilight, a very lonely heart landscape. Inevitably, I dance the suffocating void dance of the absence of a time.

가을 줍기

Autumn pick-up

그 저녁 굴뚝새는 어디로 갔나?
어깨동무 골목길은 초승달 데리고 어디로 갔나?
바람이 묻고 낙엽이 답했다.
저 언덕 너머도 내 노래 안쪽이니
이 세상 어디선가 지친 영혼들을 다독이고 있으리.

Where did the chimney bird go in the evening?
Where did the shoulder alley go take the crescent
moon?
The wind asked and the fallen leaves answered.
Even beyond that hill, inside my song.
Somewhere in the world, They will comfort the tired
souls.

소리의 흔적
Traces of the sound

잠 못 드는 적막이 벌떡 일어나 탕, 탕, 지팡이로 보름달
을 두드리는 소리의 흔적이여, 그대는 어찌하여 이렇듯
사무치는 세계 내 존재가 되는가?

Traces of the sound of a sleepless silence waking up
and tapping on the full moon with sticks bangs, bangs,
how do you become a longing being in the world?

그날 문득
Suddenly on that day

그날 문득
나뭇잎이 흰 구름을 데리고 길바닥에 쏟아졌다.

그날 문득
죽은 나뭇가지 끝에서 아버지가 쏟아졌다.

On that day, suddenly
Leaves poured down on the street with white clouds.

On that day, suddenly
Father poured out from the end of the dead branch.

기도처럼

Like a prayer

내 어머니 원족遠足 떠나시고,

밤 열두시가 밤 열두시 등에 업혀
호박잎에 내리는 빗소리 듣는 동안

하얀 의자 홀로 남으시고,

My mother's gone far away.

12 o'clock at night, on 12 o'clock at night back
While listening to the sound of rain falling on the
pumpkin leaves,

The white chair alone.

내 노래 끝 구절

The last verse of my song

지워지는 흔적이 기억이라면
덧나는 흔적은 추억인 것

시린 실개천이 내 노래 끝 구절에
흰 구름 몇 송이 풀어놓는다.

If a trace being erased is a memory
The painful trail is a wet memory

Cold brook let go some white clouds
On the last verse of my song.

힘든 날
Hard days

낙엽은 하늘이 내게 보낸 간절한 편지일 터.

미안하구나, 너무 애먹이고 가는구나, 힘든 날 많았지만
기쁜 날도 있었지.

Fallen leaves must be a desperate letter from heaven
to me.

I'm sorry, sweetheart, you've been struggling a lot,
but we've been happy days.

느닷없는 해일

An unexpected tidal wave

마지막 술잔을 비우며 이래도 한 세상 저래도 한 평생 주
섬주섬 윤심덕을 추스를 때 돈도 명예도 사랑도 다 싫다
무겁게 덮치던 그대 눈물, 그것은 느닷없는 해일이었다.
선운사 뒤뜰 휘영청 달빛이 잃어버린 시간 아득한 거기
현해탄 푸른 물을 엎질렀던 것.

It was an unexpected tidal wave, when you spent
all your life calm down Yoon Sim-deok, who drank
the last glass and hated money, honor, and love. The
time when the moonlight was lost in the backyard of
Seonun Temple, I spilled the blue water of Hyeon-
haetan.

멀리 내다보는 창문
A far-sighted window

서쪽을 멀리 내다보는 창문은 중중重重의 무게와 현현玄
玄의 깊이를 이미 알아챘다는 눈치다. 다시 못 올 어디론
가 떠날 차표를 예매해 놓고 뒤척이는 가난한 연인들의
한 평생 같은, 외로움에 겨워 허공에 붙박인, 달과 나무의
머나먼 전생을 창문은 이미 알아챘다는 눈치다.

The window, which looks far to the west, seems to
have already recognized the weight of 重重 and the
depth of 玄玄. The window seems to have already
noticed the distant past life of the moon and the trees,
stuck in the air in loneliness, like a lifetime of poor
lovers who book tickets to leave somewhere they
can't come again.

갈매기 식당

Seagull restaurant

충무시 동호동 눈 내리는 선창가에 갈매기 식당은 없다. 아무리 헤맨다 해도 도다리쑥국으로 이름난 그 식당은 한려수도 어디에도 없다. 첫사랑 무덤을 하염없이 쓰다듬는 검은 외투의 실루엣, 구름을 쟁기질하는 그대 기억 속의 갈매기 식당은, 발밑까지 쫓아와 한숨을 부려놓는 파도 소리나 괭이갈매기 울음 속에 있으리라는 게 내 생각이다.

There is no seagull restaurant in the snowy dock of Dongho-dong, Chungmu-si. No matter how many times you wander, the restaurant famous for its Dodari mugwort soup is nowhere to be found. The silhouette of a black coat stroking the first love tomb, and the seagull restaurant in your memory of plowing clouds, I think it will be in the sound of waves chasing under your feet and sighing, or in the cries of a hoe seagull.

쟁기질

Ploughing

오직 그대 삶의 쟁기질에 따라 추억은 죽임의 총구가 되고, 살림의 보습이 되기도 한다. 그럼에도 불구하고 어떤 나무는 구름 위에 두고 온 맨발 때문에 허공에 머리 두고 밤낮없이 서성인다.

Depending on the plough of your life, memories can be a gun for killing and a plough for saving. Nevertheless, some trees hang around day and night with their heads in the air because of their bare feet on the clouds.

그믐밤
Black night

싸락눈 내렸겠다.

내 새끼 이마 위에 물수건 갈아 얹는

울 엄마 가슴 새까맣게 태웠겠다.

내 새끼 훨훨 집 떠난 지 오래

울 엄마 그믐밤 홀로 지키겠다.

싸락눈 싸락싸락 내리겠다. 새하얀 알약처럼

It must have come down snow grains.

Putting a wet towel one by one on my baby's forehead

My mom must have burned her heart black.

It's been a long time since my baby left home

My mom shall keep the black night alone.

It's going to snow grains quietly. Like a white pill

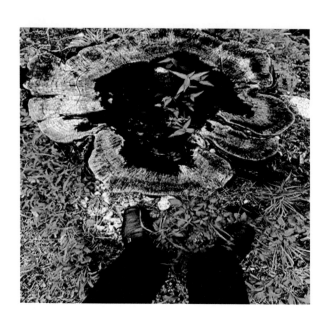

서산 마을
A mountain village in the west

세월이란 말의 서산 마을엔
까만 딱정벌레가 옹기종기 모여 산다.

그때 그날은 어느덧이고
기다림은 언제나 아직도이다.

언어의 낙타 등을 타고 가야 하리라.

In the mountain village west of the word time,
Black beetles huddle together.

That's when the day already.
Waiting is always still.

We will have to ride a language camel and so on.

왜 그토록 어려웠을까?

Why was it so difficult?

잔잔해진 눈으로 뒤돌아보는 청춘은 너무나 짧고 아름다
웠다. 젊은 날에는 왜 그것이 보이지 않았을까. (박경리)

The youth looking back with calm eyes was so short
and beautiful. "Why didn't I see it when I was young?"
(Park Kyung-ri)

나는 내 속에서 스스로 솟아 나오르려는 것, 바로 그것
을 살아보려 했다. 그것이 왜 그토록 어려웠을까?(헤르
만 헷세)

I tried to live just it, what was trying to rising out of me
by himself. Why was it so difficult? (Hermann Hesse)

이쯤 와서 생각하니

Now that I think about it

그토록 많은 폐허 위에
그토록 많은 추억 위에 시간은 멈추었다.
너에게 이르러 긴장을 푸는 그 길의 끝이 그리운 밤
덜덜거리던 삶의 시동을 끄고, 이쯤 와서 생각하니
인생은 짧은 만남, 긴 이별의 정거장이었다.

On so many ruins

Time stopped on so many memories.

The night I miss the end of the road to relax arrived
at you

I've turned off my shaky life, and now that I've come
to think about it

Life was a stop of short meeting, long farewell.

적막한 상형문자
Silent hieroglyphs

하늘을 두루마리 삼고
바다를 먹물 삼아도 다 쓰지 못하는 궁핍의 서사

아린 이승의 손끝으로 새긴
적막한 상형문자, 어머니!

With the sky as a scroll
A narrative of poverty that cannot be used even if the
sea is used as ink

Engraved with the bitter fingertips of this world
Silent hieroglyphics, Mother!

조그만 책상 서랍
Small desk drawer

눈 나라에는 꿈꾸기 좋은 구석방이 있고, 종이비행기가
날아다니는 조그만 책상 서랍이 있고, 서랍 속에는 노란
은행잎과 서양 나라에서 보내온 크리스마스카드가 있고.
북 치는 소년이 어서 와! 나를 부르고 있고…

In the snow country, there are corner rooms that are
good for dreams, small desk drawers where paper
airplanes fly, and in the drawers are yellow ginkgo
leaves and Christmas cards sent from Western coun-
tries. Welcome, the boy who beats the drums! He's
calling me…

하얀 통곡

White wailing

남루한 세월로 가득한 아버지!

자책의 창끝이 옆구리를 찔렀다.

하얀 통곡이 쇳물처럼 쏟아졌다.

A father full of boring years!

The tip of the spear of self-blame pierced his side.

White wailing poured out like molten iron.

저 구름 흘러가는 곳

Wherethe clouds flow

용서
Forgiveness

싸우다 귀를 찢긴 고양이처럼, 산비탈을 헐떡이는 기차처럼 내 속의 지친 나를 불러내어 술 한 잔 권하고 싶을 때가 있다. 꽃이 지거나, 저녁놀이 곱거나, 물안개 자욱할 때가 그러하다. 내 마음속에 발 뻗는 기억들이 옷 찢는 회한이든, 치솟는 분노이든, 그 또한 여기까지 함께 온 나의 반려이니 그동안 애썼다고 어깨를 다독이며 내가 나에게 예의를 갖추고 싶을 때가 있는 것이다.
소식 없는 내 사랑 무심한 목소리로 우는 소리 들릴 때…

There are times when I want to call me up for a drink, like a cat that tore its ears while fighting, like a train panting on the hillside. This is the case when flowers are falling, sunset glow is beautiful, or water fog is thick. Whether the memories that stretch out in my heart are regrettable tear apart clothes or soaring anger, there are times when I want to be polite to myself, saying that I've been working hard because I'm my companion who came all the way here

가락지
A ring

우리라는 말은 가락지 같다.
너와 나를 꼭 조이는 가락지 같다.
가락지 사이 뒤척이는 먼바다
당신을 기다리는 외로운 등대

The word "we" is like a ring.
It's like a ring that tightens you and me.
The distant sea that flips between the rings.
A lonely lighthouse waiting for you.

강둑을 덮다
Cover a riverbank

흐르는 강이 흐르지 않는 것은
저문 날이 저문 강을 데려갔기 때문이다.

돌계단에 엎질러진 당신 눈물이
붉게 더욱 붉게 강둑을 덮는 것은
내가 강둑으로 누워 있기 때문이다.

The reason why the flowing river doesn't flow
This is because the day of sunset took the river.

Your tears that fell on the stone steps
To cover the riverbank with redder
Because I'm lying down like a riverbank

구병산 저 너머

Beyond Gubyeongsan

구병산 저 너머엔 누가 살고 있을까. 구병산 이마 위에 걸린 저녁노을이 다 익어서 붉다가 제 마음에 겨워 어두워지면 은행잎 노랗게 흩날리는 거기, 단발머리 소녀가 마루 끝에 나와 앉아 별똥별 하나 둘 세고 있겠다.

Who lives beyond Gubyungsan? The sunset on the forehead of Gubyungsan is ripe and red, and when it gets dark in its heart, there ginkgo leaves fall yellow, the short-haired girl will be sitting at the end of the floor and counting shooting stars one by one.

그럼에도 불구하고
Nevertheless

비비추 새순처럼 그리움 치솟거든 봄비 맞으며 나 온 줄
알아라.
그럼에도 불구하고
창가에 촛불처럼 타오르는 내 마음, 바람 부는 그곳으로
천리를 간다.

If your longing soars like a hosta new shoot think that
I came out in the spring rain.
Nevertheless
My heart burning by the window like a candle, I go to
the windy place endlessly.

그리움이 구부린

Bent in longing

그리움은 먼 길이 구부린 것이고
먼 길은 그리움이 구부린 것이다.

당신이 꿈꿀 때 당신은 그 꿈이 된다.

Longing is the bent by a long way
A long way is the bent by a longing.

When you dream, you become that dream.

기다림에 대해

About waiting

그럼에도 불구하고 꽃이 핀다면 그리운 사람이 돌아온
것이다.
그럼에도 불구하고 꽃이 진다면 그리운 사람이 떠난 것
이다.

Nevertheless, if flowers bloom, the person you miss
is back.
Nevertheless, if the flowers fall, the person you miss
has left.

꿈틀거린다

Wriggle

정지할 수 없는 어떤 기막힘이 있어

봄이 왔다, 큰일 났다.
가난한 내 사랑도 꿈틀거린다.

There's something a loss for words that can't stop so

Spring has come, I'm in trouble.
Even my poor love is wriggling too.

그림

펜으로 그림을 그리는 건 취미가 아니야, 삶이야.

무엇을 그리는 게 아니라 그려지는 무엇을 그리는 거지.

—김개미

개미의 펜 끝
The tip of an ant's pen

개미의 펜 끝에서 내가 태어났다.

내 발끝에서 개미가 태어났다.

태어난다는 건 취미가 아니야, 삶이야

내가 태어나는 게 아니라 태어나서 내가 되는 거지.

I was born at the end of an ant's pen.

An ant was born at the end of my foot.

Being born is not a hobby, it's a life.

I'm not born, I'm born to be me.

능소화 폭염

A trumpet creeper heat wave

오지 않는 사람을 기다리는 여름이었다.
기다리는 내 마음이 길바닥에 달라붙어 징징거렸다.

It was a summer waiting for those who didn't come.
My waiting heart was clinging to the street and whin-
ing.

도마뱀 부부

Lizard couple

지붕을 헐었다. 꼬리에 못 박힌 도마뱀 한 마리가 두 눈 멀뚱멀뚱 살아있다. 도마뱀 한 마리가 먹이를 물어와 건 네준다. 지붕은 마저 헐리고 도마뱀 부부는 그 집을 떠 났다.

The roof was torn down. A lizard with a nail on its tail is alive with its eyes are wide open. A lizard picks up food and hands it over. The roof was completely torn down and the lizard couple left the house.

뜨개질
Knitting

가난한 내 사랑은 저 강을 건너간 것이어서 소식조차 없
을 때
사무치는 손끝이 한숨과 체념의 실을 꿰어 뜨개질을 하
고 있었으리라.
기약 없이 눈 내리는 그믐밤,
이따금 개 짖는 소리가 동구 밖 적막을 일깨우는 외딴 집
이었으리라.

When my poor love crossed that river and I didn't
even hear from you
Too much fingertips must have been knitting with
thread of sigh and resignation.
Last night, when it snowed without any promise,
It must have been a remote house that the barking of
a dog awakens silence in outside village from time to
time.

먼 곳으로 출렁이는

Swaying far away

새싹이 돋는 아픔을 지나, 바람과 햇볕과 부푼 흙의 수런
거림을 지나,
둥근 열매들의 허공에 이르기까지! 먼 곳으로 출렁이는
논둑길처럼.

Passing through the pain of sprouts, through the
wind, sunlight, and swollen soil,
To the air of the round fruits! Like a rice paddy path
that floats far away.

메아리처럼
Like an echo

그대 눈빛 속에는
감꽃 피고 지는 시간의 집이 있지.
멀리멀리 갔다가 허기져 돌아온 메아리처럼
그대 눈빛 속에는
천리를 뒤척이는 언 발의 꿈이 있지.

In your eyes
There's a home of persimmon blossom and fall time
Like an echo that went far and came back hungry
In your eyes
A frozen feet dream of tossing and turning is in it far-
away

문득 멈춘 저녁노을

The sunset that suddenly stopped

수면제가 삼켜버린 바다
수면제를 삼켜버린 바다

누가 제 몸을 불살라 번제를 드리는지

바다는 없고
통곡소리 문득 멈춘 저녁노을뿐

Sea swallowed by sleeping pills

The sea that swallowed sleeping pills

Who's gonna burn his body for burnt offerings

There's no sea

It's just the sunset that suddenly stopped wailing

편지
Letter

내려오는 기차 안에서 왜 뜬금없이 선생님 생각이 났을
까?
궁금했지만, 그때 선생님 생각을 한 사람은 온데간데 없
어져
답을 듣진 못했습니다. 2020. 11. 17.

Why did I suddenly think of you on the train coming
down?
I was wondering, but the man who thought of you at
the time gone.
I didn't hear the answer. 2020. 11. 17

봄날은 간다
Spring goes

기다림이 저 혼자
흘러 흘러서 바다에 닿는 동안

제 몸속에 팔다리를 구겨 넣은 돌멩이처럼
사라진 먼 곳처럼 감꽃이 피는 동안

Awaiting alone
While it flows and it touches the sea

Like a rock with his limbs crumpled himself
While the persimmon flower blooms like a faraway
that has disappeared

세월이 가도

Even if time goes by

떠나는 소리는 왜 때가 묻지 않는지?

적막한 칼끝은 왜 녹이 슬지 않는지?

그리움은 왜 나이를 먹지 않는지?

Why doesn't the sound of goodbye get dirty?

Why doesn't the desolate tip of the knife rust?

Why doesn't longing get older?

사모곡

Song for my mother

꽃 피면 눈물 나서
눈물 속에 꽃 피어서

당신은 어디 계신지?
환하게 열리는 연분홍 서쪽

When flowers bloom in tears
In tears in bloom

Where are you?
Open brightly west of the soft pink

빗장을 여는 그대

You who open the latch

그대 손길이 있어 가지 끝에 떨고 있는 외로움이 털 장갑을 낀 추억이 되듯, 캄캄한 겨울밤 지옥의 행군도 그대 눈빛으로 출구를 찾는다.

Just as the loneliness that trembles at the tip of a branch with your hand becomes a memory wearing woolen gloves, the march to hell on a dark winter night finds an exit with your eyes.

우리 오빠 말 타고

My brother by horse

fort-

빨간 구두 사가지고 오신다더니!

da-

fort-

You said you'd bring red shoes!

da-

저 구름 흘러가는 곳
Where the clouds are going

저 구름 흘러가는 서쪽은 바보
해종일 귀 막고 그대 소식 기다리네.

창문도 닫지 않고, 찬바람 어쩌라고
마음이 몸속을 들락거리네.

The west side of that cloud flows is a fool
I've been covering my ears all day and waiting to hear
from you.

You don't close the windows, you don't want the cold
wind
My heart is going in and out of my body.

흙과 놀다
Play with the soil

어둠이 어둑어둑 울밑으로 잦아들었다.
장에 간 우리 어무이 왜 안 오시나?

흙빛은 아무 일도 없는 흙빛이어서
동구 밖 초승달이 애틋했다.

The dark faded into the fence dark and dark.
Why isn't my mother coming from the market?

The color of the soil is the color of the soil that nothing happened
The crescent moon outside the village entrance was
sorrowful.

정처

Destination

정처 없는 이 발길이 찾아가는 정처는 세상에 없다.
길 위의 시간, 길 위의 이 발길이 정처일 뿐이다.

There is no destination in the world where this aim-
less visit is found.
The time on the road, this way on the road, is just the
destination.

구름의 책가방

A school bag of the clouds

책가방이 없어, 문맹인 구름이

몸이 없어 몸무게가 없는 구름이

날개뿐인 구름이, 현현玄玄한 저 구름이

이윽고 떠나왔으므로 떠나온 먼 곳으로 이윽고 돌아가

야 할

평평平平한 무심 축제!

No school bag, illiterate clouds

Without body, a cloud without body weight

Clouds have only wings, far away that clouds

We've come a long way and we've come a long way

and we've got to go back

Calm and silent festival!